LITTLE MISS SCARY

Roger Hargreaves

D1512966

Written and illustrated by
Adam Hargreaves

EGMONT

Little Miss Scary lived near the top of a mountain in a house called Spooky Cottage.

When it was dark she would creep into the valley below, making sure that nobody saw her …

… and there she would wait very quietly until somebody came along …

… and when that somebody did, she would tiptoe up behind them, open her mouth wide, and shout …

"BOO!"

And do you know why Little Miss Scary did this?

For fun.

You see, she loved to scare people more than anything else in the world.

And she was very good at it.

She scared them stiff.

"BOO!"

She scared them out of their wits.

"BOO!"

She even scared them right out of their socks.

"BOO!"

About a week ago, Mr Noisy went to see his friend Mr Jelly.

Mr Noisy was worried because he hadn't heard from his friend for ages.

When he got to Mr Jelly's house, he knocked on the door.

Spookily, the door swung open by itself.

"HELLO," called Mr Noisy as softly as he could, which for you or me would have been a shout.

Then he heard a chattering noise coming from the bedroom.

Mr Noisy found Mr Jelly hiding under his bed, his teeth chattering in fear.

"WHATEVER'S THE ..." began Mr Noisy, and then remembered himself. "Whatever's the matter, Mr Jelly?"

"It's ... it's ... L-L-Little Miss S-S-Scary," chattered Mr Jelly, trembling in fear. "Sh-sh-she keeps jumping out and shouting 'B-b-b-boo' at me."

Mr Noisy made Mr Jelly a cup of tea, calmed him down, and told him what they were going to do.

Just as it was getting dark, they hid behind a bush beside the lane that led up to Mr Jelly's house.

They waited until they saw Little Miss Scary's shadowy figure creeping past them.

Then Mr Noisy and Mr Jelly crept out from their hiding place, tiptoed up behind Little Miss Scary and, at the tops of their voices, shouted …

"BOO!"

Now, the top of Mr Noisy's voice is a very loud place indeed.

So loud that Little Miss Scary leapt five feet in the air, and when she came down she ran for her life.

She didn't stop running until she was hidden under her bed.

In her bedroom.

In Spooky Cottage.

At the top of the mountain.

"I don't think you'll be seeing so much of her for a long while, Mr Jelly," chuckled Mr Noisy.

"Mr Jelly? Mr Jelly …?"

But there was no sign of Mr Jelly either.

Mr Noisy chuckled again, and walked back to Mr Jelly's house.

To have a look under Mr Jelly's bed!